MĀUI,
MISCHIEVOUS
HERO

MĀUI,
MISCHIEVOUS
HERO

By Barbara Baldwin Lyons
illustrations by Dietrich Varez

Publisher's Note

These traditional stories of the demi-god Māui, retold by the late Barbara Baldwin Lyons, were originally printed in The Maui News and The Honolulu Advertiser. They were collected into the first edition of Māui, Mischievous Hero and published by Petroglyph Press in 1969. This second edition presents her folktales combined with the art of the late Dietrich Varez, whose block prints also celebrate this Hawaiian folk hero. They were both avid students of Hawaiian culture and shared a passion for the folklore and storytelling arts of Hawai'i and Polynesia.

Māui, Mischievous Hero
by Barbara Baldwin Lyons
Dedication: For Roger and Michelle, Wendy and Philip

First Edition Copyright 1969 by Petroglyph Press, Ltd.
Second Edition Copyright 2022
Illustrations Copyright 2022 Dietrich and Linda Varez Trust
Book Design by Krystal Meisel
Mahalo to Karen Kaufman of Mo Media for the cover art colorization and other art services.

All Rights Reserved

ISBN 978-0-912180-80-9

Published in Hilo, Hawai'i
www.PetroglyphPress.com

CONTENTS

MĀUI, MISCHIEVOUS HERO

Perhaps the most dearly loved of the Polynesian Gods is Māui, born of Hina for whom the moon was named. Māui the quickest one, the mischief maker, benefactor, worker of miracles. Tales of his exploits have been told for so many centuries that no one can know when he really lived. But surely he was a real man, remarkable enough to have occasioned the relating of his achievements, which in time gave him the status of deity. The Māori of New Zealand say that he helped other gods to create man.

He must have been a great voyager and explorer, for he was known to so many islands of the Pacific. His fame traveled to places that he could never have reached, places of which he became a legendary part through the accounts repeated down the ages by men whose ancestors had known of him.

Probably the reason Māui is so well loved is his mixture of human and godlike qualities. As a demigod he had supernatural power which he used to benefit his race; but he loved, too, to play pranks, and like some other men was accused of neglecting his family. His brothers professed to scorn him, but were impressed in spite of themselves by his magical acts. These were many, and were performed from the time he was a young boy. Best known among them are *The Seven Great Deeds of Māui*. Following are versions of these stories told on the island of Maui, with one adapted from the Māori legend.

MĀUI SEEKS HIS HOME

When Hina's fifth son was born, he was so little and scrawny that she didn't think he could possibly be alive, and she threw him into the sea. She had four fine boys already, and none of them had ever been so small and wizened as this one. She felt sad, for she knew that this fifth boy would have grown into a very special kind of person.

But the baby was, after all, alive, and it wasn't long before some jellyfish found him floating on the water near shore. They took him to their home beneath the waves, and there they cared for and mothered him. They were so kind that he was quite happy with them. But one day, the god of the sea swam by.

"What's this?" he said. "A boy? Where in the sea did you find him?"

The jellyfish explained, and the sea god said, "A boy who can live in the water must be a god. I think I'll take him home with me."

The jellyfish were very sorry to hear this, but still they realized what an honor was being bestowed upon their little charge. They bade him a loving farewell, and asked him to come back to see them sometimes.

The sea god took him to his home in a cave at the edge of the sea.

"What shall I call you?" he mused.

"I seem to know that my name is Māui," the boy replied. "And that my father is a god."

As he grew older, Māui felt as much at home swimming and playing in the water as he did on land. He came to know all of the creatures of the sea, and they were his friends. Now and then he went to the jellyfish's home, and he was always glad to see them. Still he was lonely at times, for there were no other boys to join in his play. And he longed sometimes for a mother.

He began to wonder about his family, and asked the sea god if he might go in search of them.

"You are too young to go off alone," the god replied. "Besides, think of me. I'd be very lonesome without you."

Māui did think of the kindly god who had befriended him, and hated to hurt him. Yet he knew that someday he must leave. He waited for what seemed a very long time. Until he had grown taller, and asked again.

He saw the sadness in the god's eyes as he answered, "You are old enough now, Māui. If this is still what you want, then go."

The boy tried to tell his old friend of all that was in his heart, how grateful he was for the care he had received, and how in one way he wanted to stay. But all he could do was to stand before the god with bowed head.

The other seemed to understand. Laying his hand on the boy's head, he said, "The time has come for you to go. But we'll remember each other, won't we?"

"Oh, yes!" cried the boy. "Always."

He went to where the jellyfish lived, and they took him to the place where they had found him and said, "Your home must be near."

Māui went from one village to another, and everywhere he asked, "Is there any mother here who thought her baby was dead, and threw him into the sea?"

This question was received by puzzled stares, and sometimes by laughter. Once he saw a woman so beautiful that he hoped it might be her. But when he asked her, she tossed her head and replied, "Not me. You must really have been pathetic looking, to have your mother throw you away."

Māui walked on, feeling sad, and thinking that the ocean's tide might have swept him a long way before the jellyfish rescued him. Would he ever find his home? The sun had set and it was nearly dark, and he wondered where he would sleep.

From the distance, he heard a strain of music, and as he looked in its direction a light appeared. It glimmered through the dusk of twilight, and seemed to beckon him ...

When he reached it, he saw that it came from the doorway of a house where people had gathered to sing and dance. How gay they looked! It was dark now and he stayed there unseen, beyond the stream of light. Then his heart missed a beat. A woman stood across the room, and she was his mother! How he knew this so surely, he couldn't tell. But he was certain. She looked kind, and so pretty, and comfortable.

Just the way a mother should look, thought Māui.

And those four boys - they must be his brothers. They were all bigger than Māui, and they were laughing and talking together in a way that made Māui feel very much alone. He just stood there in the darkness, watching.

When his mother and the boys left, Māui followed them, hiding behind trees and ferns along the way so they wouldn't see him. He found that they lived in a set of grass houses beside a waterfall.

Māui found some berries to eat, and went silently past the house where the family slept, to drink from a pool. He felt spray from the waterfall on his back, cool and delicious.

How peaceful the house looked, with the moon rising beyond it and silvering the thatch of the roof and the coconut fronds nearby. If only he could sleep there with them all! Be a member of a family... He gathered ferns for his bed, and slept as near the house as he dared.

In the morning, Māui watched from behind a tree as his brothers played. How he'd love to join in their game! Engrossed, he drew closer. After a time, one of the boys noticed him.

"Who are you?" he asked.

Māui gathered his courage and said, "I'm your brother!"

"Do you expect us to believe that?" the other asked. "Our brother was born dead, and our mother threw him into the sea." The boys looked at each other and laughed at him for telling such a story.

"I wasn't dead!" cried Māui. "And I am your brother. My name is Māui. Can't you see that I look like you?" He had seen his reflection only in a smooth black stone held in a calabash of water, and sometimes in a quiet pool, but he thought - he hoped - it was true. "Our fathers are not the same, but your mother – she's mine, too!"

The brothers paid no attention to this, and just went on with their play. They were playing Warrior, a game in which they used spears made of sugar cane stalks.

The biggest of the boys looked the nicest, Māui decided. After a while, he approached him and said, "Will you let me play with you? I love to play Warrior, but I've always had to play it by myself."

The boy hesitated, and before he had time to reply another scoffed, "You play with us? You're not big enough!"

Just then the mother went by on her way to the little house where she beat mulberry bark into tapa cloth.

Māui ran up to her and said, "Don't you remember me?"

"No, I don't know you," she answered, glancing at him carelessly. "Whose boy are you?"

"I'm your boy!" Māui cried eagerly.

But she only replied, "Don't be silly, what an idea," and turned away.

One of the boys said, "Well, if you are our brother, you ought to be a good Warrior player." He smiled at the others, and they all laughed.

"Yes, let him try!" they said jeeringly.

Quickly Māui began to fashion a spear from one of the cane stalks.

"Let's throw our spears onto the roof," one of the boys suggested. "Or can you throw that far, Māui?" he added mockingly.

One by one the long stalks sailed through the air, not very fast because they were so light, and lay on the roof or rolled harmlessly off it. When Māui's turn came, the others smiled again as they watched him preparing to throw.

But Māui was saying to himself, I will show my mother that I am her son. And I'll give my brothers a surprise! He muttered a chant over his spear, placing a charm on it. Then he drew back his arm and hurled.

Swift as an arrow the spear flew, and with a tearing sound it plunged right through the roof, leaving a great gaping hole in the pili grass thatch. The boys stared at Māui, too amazed to speak. Hina came running from her tapa house.

''What has happened?" she cried. She gazed at the hole in the roof of the sleeping-house, then at the strange boy. "My son," she said softly, "I know now that you are mine. Only the son of a god could make a sugar cane spear do the work of a kauila wood one." She put her arms around him, and Māui knew at last what it was to have a mother. Three of the boys looked darkly at Māui, jealous of this new brother who had done such a miraculous thing. But the eldest said, "Come, brother, '' and led him toward the door.

LIFTER OF THE SKIES

One day, when Māui was swimming with his brothers, he lay for a long time floating on his back in the water.

''What's the matter with Māui?'' asked one of the boys. "He seems to be going to sleep."

"He's not asleep," said another. "He's just resting up while he thinks of a trick to play on us." For Māui, secure now that he had become part of a family, was quite a prankster.

He was gazing thoughtfully at the sky, through narrowed lids. He paid no attention to his brothers; he was worried, and this time was not thinking of a prank.

The others began to play a game called Fish. One of the boys was the fish and the rest, each armed with a stick, tried to spear him.

"Come on, Māui!" they called. "You can be the fish." But still he lay there, frowning up into the blue.

After a while, he turned over and swam toward his brothers. "Look at the sky," he called. "It seems to me that it's lower than usual - and getting closer all the time."

"That's funny," said one, shading his eyes with his hand and looking upward. "It *does* look closer."

"It's coming down!" cried another. "I saw it move."

Māui watched for a minute longer, then swam toward the beach. "I'm going to tell our mother about it," he called back.

At this time, Māui and his family were living at Hana, near one

end of the great mountain, Haleakalā. He hurried to their home, a group of grass houses not far from the big hill Ka'uiki, which jutted out into the water.

"Mother!" he shouted. "Come out and look at the sky!" Hina put her head out through the door of the house in which she was weaving long, slender hala leaves into straw-like lauhala. She wasn't sorry for an excuse to stop work for a bit. It was tedious, sitting there alone all day, weaving.

When she saw the sky, she gasped. It was down to the tops of the trees! "Whatever is happening?" she cried, clasping Māui's wet brown body to her and not even noticing that it was making her tapa dress damp. "Oh, what shall we do?" Perhaps Hina herself didn't realize it, but she was beginning to rely on her youngest son, trickster though he was.

"Maybe it has stopped," Māui said. "Let's wait and see."

But the sky hadn't stopped.

Every minute it came closer, until it nearly touched the earth. Hina and Māui had to get down on their hands and knees, and soon the brothers came crawling from the beach.

"Don't worry, Mother," Māui was saying consolingly. "I'll think of a way to get the sky back where it belongs."

His brothers only laughed. "What can you do about it?" they jeered.

For days all the people had to go about on their knees, and it became very tiresome. It was hot, for there was no room for the trade winds to blow. And it was dark, for clouds filled the narrow space between earth and sky. The trees were pressed down, and their leaves flattened by the weight of the sky.

At last Māui said, "This is too much. We must put a stop to it - and I have an idea."

He remembered having heard of an old woman who kept a special kind of water in her calabash, water that could give a man great strength. Where did she live? It was under the brow of a hill - yes, that was it. If only he could find her in this clouded atmosphere!

Off he went, as fast as he could on hands and knees, and at last came to her house.

"Please, Old Woman," he said excitedly, "let me have some of your magic water, for I believe that with its help I can do something about the sky."

"Wait a minute – not so fast," she said. "Who are you?"

He told her, and she said, considering him, "You're not a bad looking boy. But one would hardly think you were big enough to do much about the sky, even after a drink of my magic water. What makes you think you can?"

Māui smiled at her sweetly, and said only, "Won't you let me try?"

"Well, perhaps there's no harm in that. You're just a boy, but the water is powerful. And anything for a chance to stand again!" She went into her house and returned with a large koa wood calabash.

Māui drank deeply, and felt strength flowing into his body and along his arms and legs. The old woman watched as he put up his hands and pushed against the sky. It moved, just a little!

"Thank you, Old Woman!" he cried. "Now, look at this!"

Up, up drifted the clouds - up over the tree-tops! The trees again stood straight and tall, but their leaves remained flat, as they have been ever since.

"My, you are strong," the old woman commented.

"See what I'm going to do next!" he boasted.

Quickly he ran to Ka'uiki Hill, climbed it and, with his back, arched the sky. With a last mighty heave, he thrust it far above the top of Haleakalā. Then, with either hand, he drew down the edges of the sky to the horizon.

"Good for you!" said Hina, when he reached home.

"Not bad," his oldest brother remarked, but one of the others added, "I was just about to think of doing that myself."

Sometimes now clouds hover over the mountains, or lie in a long heavy bank across the slopes of Haleakalā. But they always disperse before too long, for fear Māui will return and raise them so high that they will never find their way back.

THE BIGGEST FISH OF ALL

Māui loved to go with his brothers in their canoe when they went fishing. But he scarcely ever caught a fish, and was apt to do mischievous things like rocking the boat. Finally, the others decided that they had had enough of Māui as a fisherman.

"You just take up room in the canoe," they said. "And you're a nuisance to us with your tricks. Stay home with our mother, and perhaps she can find something useful for you to do."

Māui felt very sad at being left behind, and he didn't want to do a woman's work. He hid from his mother by climbing a tall coconut tree and snuggling down among the long green fronds at its top.

Hina called to him, but when he didn't answer, went back to her chores.

As he lay there in his secret green place, with a breeze from the sea gently stirring the fronds and cooling him, he thought about fish hooks. It seemed to him that with another sort of fishhook, many more fish could be caught. Māui hadn't forgotten that the sea creatures had befriended him, but now that he was older and would soon be a man, he realized that people must fish in order to live. And he knew that he could always warn the ones that were his special friends.

If there were something about a hook that made it harder for the fish to slip off ... Yes, that was what was needed. After a while, he slid down the slim trunk of the palm and went to the place where his family kept bone and other materials for making their tools and weapons. He searched about for a bit and found a likely looking curved bone, which he cut to the length he wanted with a piece of flaked stone. Then he picked up a coral rasp and set to work at smoothing the bone and shaping it into a hook that he thought would hold the fish. It was a quite new design - a fish hook with a barb.

The next morning, when the brothers were ready to start off in their canoe, Māui went up to them eagerly and showed them what he held in his hand. "It's a new kind of fishhook," he explained. "See, it has a barb, and it should catch lots more fish than the kind you've been using."

H'm, said the brothers. "Well, well. Give it here and we'll try it out."

Did they mean to go without him when he had made this new hook for them? "Let me come, too!" cried Māui.

"Oh, you," the others said. "You couldn't catch a mullet in the king's fish pond - even if this does prove to be a good hook, which we doubt."

It was, in fact, a very good hook indeed, and the brothers returned with their canoe loaded with fish. But still, they wouldn't take Māui with them when they went again.

Māui was hurt about this, when it was he who had fashioned the splendid new hook. He resolved to show his brothers that he was really the best fisherman of all and he thought he knew how he could do it. He had heard of an ancestress of his who lived in the underworld, who was dead on one side and alive on the other. If only she will agree to what I want, Māui thought, I will be able to make a magic fishhook.

He went on the dark, frightening journey to the underworld, and there in a great, gloomy cavern he found his ancestress.

"Old Woman," he said, "I beg you to give me a bone from your jaw on the side of you that is dead, so that I can make a magic fishhook." He told her who he was and of how his brothers had behaved, and that he wanted to prove that he too could fish.

24

"Is this so important to you, boy?" She sat looking him up and down as he stood before her, straight and as tall as he could make himself.

"It's the most important thing in life to me, right now. And I'll tell you a secret. The fish I catch with my magic hook will be like none ever caught before."

The old woman grinned. "I love secrets," she said. "I'll remember that." There was a gleam of kindness in her ancient eye as she added, "You're a nice boy, and of my family. I will give you what you ask." She took a bone from her jaw, on the dead side.

"Oh, thank you, my Ancestress! You won't be sorry, when you hear of the fish this has caught."

He went back up into the world of light, and made his fishhook. Then he sought his mother.

Oh, Hina, dear mother, I have made a magic fishhook, but I need bait for it. Will you let me have one of your sacred 'alae birds?"

Hina knew that Māui was capable of making a magic hook, because his father was a god. "Yes, son," she said, "I will give you a nice fat one." She picked a bird out from under the great wooden calabash where she kept her sacred 'alae, and Māui hid it beneath his malo, the brief garment he wore.

Then he ran to his brothers, who were about to go off in the canoe. "Let me go with you," he called.

But they shoved off without him and he stood at the edge of the sea, hearing their laughter float back to him and watching as the canoe grew smaller and smaller. At last it was hidden by the waves. Standing in water to his knees, Māui uttered a chant, sending a message to the kinds of fish his brothers hoped to catch.

The fishermen came home early this time, discouraged because they had found nothing but sharks. Māui could have told them why.

"I will show you where the biggest fish of all is," he said. "Set out again, and take me along."

"All right," said the eldest. "Why not, brothers? There's still plenty of daylight left, and perhaps he will really show us where Pimoe and the ulua are."

Māui urged them on and on, farther and farther beyond the reef, until the ocean was a very dark blue. Waves splashed over the side of the canoe, and when they looked toward shore, Haleakalā was a long, low mound, pale and far away. The brothers were frightened; never had they paddled out so far. "Let's go back now," they said. "Māui is playing a joke on us."

"No, wait," Māui said. He baited his magic hook with the 'alae and let the line fall into the water. Down, down it went, until it must have reached the bottom of the sea. There it caught fast on something.

Now the brothers were excited. They paddled with all their strength, and said, "Māui must have hooked the biggest fish in the ocean!" How heavy the fish was - would they ever pull it from the depths of the sea?

When the canoe was lifted by an enormous swell, the boys had to paddle furiously to keep the craft upright. After the wave had gone by and they could see it rippling on into the distance, one of the brothers, exhausted, paused to look back. He gave a cry of terror.

When the others turned, it was to see a new island floating on the sea behind them.

THE SUN THAT TRAVELED TOO FAST

At one time Māui lived with his mother and brothers at Makalia, near the very end of Mauna Kahālāwai, the Meeting Place between Heaven and Earth. This mountain thrust into the sea, and from its tip one looked across the water to great, soaring Haleakalā, House of the Sun.

The boys spent most of their time in the water, swimming and fishing, but Hina was kept busy making tapa cloth for her family. The boys wore only malo most of the time, it was true, and they didn't take much material. But tapa was needed for blankets, too and it seemed to Hina that they had to be replaced entirely too often.

"You boys are so rough!" she complained. "And sometimes you go to bed with dirty hands and feet. Tapa won't wash, you know."

"We'll be more careful, Mother," Māui promised. He put his nose to her cheek and sniffed, the Hawaiian way of kissing.

"Sentimental this morning, aren't you?" Hina gave him an affectionate cuff. "The main trouble is," she went on, "the days are getting so short that my tapa simply hasn't time to dry. That old sun travels across the sky faster each day, it seems to me as if he just couldn't wait to get to bed."

Māui noticed after this that the sun did seem to sail through the heavens very swiftly indeed. In the mornings, Hina went to her mulberry grove as soon as the first rays appeared over the rim of

Haleakalā. She tore bark from the trees, rolled up the long strips and put them to soak in calabashes of sea water. Later it must be stretched out to dry, and the outer bark scraped away with a large seashell. When Hina sat before her tapa-making house and beat the bark with a club of hard kauila wood, she would pray to the goddess of tapa beaters. This was the goddess who had changed herself into the first mulberry tree, that her people might have tapa.

But these days, the sun was ready to sink down into the underworld long before Hina's cloth had had time to dry.

"It's so discouraging," she cried, and Māui saw that this was true.

When the sun rose the next morning, he sat staring at it until he had to close his eyes. But he had noticed the long legs that were spaced evenly around the sun, shining golden upon the blue of sky. He thought, if I could snare those legs... How many are there? he wondered. He squinted, and counted. Four, five.... When he got up to eleven, he had to look away and then start again. Fifteen, he decided at last. I think it's fifteen.

All day he thought, and in the morning he set out along the slopes of Mauna Kahālāwai for the valley of Waiheʻe. Here there was a fine grove of palm trees, and from the husks of their coconuts Māui made fifteen long cords. These he took home, and told Hina of the plan that was forming in his mind.

"But the sun has sixteen legs," she said. Why hadn't he thought of asking her? Hina knew just about everything.

''You will need one more let me think."

Māui waited anxiously as she sat with furrowed brow and intent expression. At last she said, "Your grandmother lives just at the edge of Haleakalā Crater, not far from where the sun comes up in the morning. Her home is near a wiliwili tree. I'm sure she will help you."

So, carrying his fifteen strands, Māui started off early the next day on the long climb to the top of Haleakalā: Up one hill after another - it seemed as if they would never end! Always another, just beyond.

At last he reached the rocky slopes near the summit, and there, beside a great gap in the crater's side, was the wiliwili tree his mother had described. Under it sat an old woman, stringing round red wiliwili seeds onto a fine cord.

"Oh, Grandmother," Māui said, "I have come to snare the sun because he goes so fast across the sky that my mother's tapa hasn't time to dry." He showed her his long ropes of coconut fiber. "But I need one more, for his sixteenth leg - something like the cord you have there, though perhaps a bit stronger. Will you give me one, Grandmother?"

"Just wait till I finish my lei," she said, "then we'll see. Sit down, boy."

It seemed to Māui that his grandmother took forever to finish stringing that lei. Her eyes didn't seem to be very good, she bent so low over it. Well, she must be pretty old. He sat waiting quietly.

Finally, she knotted her string and looked up. "Good boy," she said. "You're lively, I can tell by the look in your eye, but still you can wait patiently." She put the lei over his head and ambled into her grass house.

When she returned, she was holding a strong cord in one hand and an ax in the other. "This is a magic ax," she told him, placing it in his hand. "It may come in handy."

Māui thanked her gratefully. As the sun was about to set in the ocean near the island of Lāna'i, she gave him some poi and breadfruit for dinner and showed him a bed of tapa blankets where he might sleep. He had to use many of the blankets to keep warm, here at the top of the mountain. It's lucky Grandmother doesn't have to make tapa for five boys, he thought as he fell asleep.

Next morning early, armed with his sixteen strands and the magic ax, he waited for the sun to wake up. No one knew just how that bright fellow got from the underworld back to the crater. Every afternoon he went down over the horizon toward the west, and in the morning he rose from the crater of Haleakalā, to the east.

Māui sat in the darkness, waiting. It was cold, and he longed for the sun's warmth. At last, a streak of light! He peered through the gap in the crater's wall, across the black sands of dead lava to the light-colored sandy hills that were volcanic cones. Above one of these he saw a leg, as if the sun were beginning to stretch. Quickly he tossed a cord and caught the leg, and fastened it to the wiliwili tree.

Another leg followed, and another, and Māui snared them. The sun looked sleepily out from behind the cone, as if he were still too drowsy to know what was happening. Leg followed leg, and finally the sun said crossly, "What do you think you're doing?"

"I know what I'm doing," Māui answered. "Catching your legs, that's what!" and he looped the sixteenth strand.

The sun was more awake now and he tried to draw back his last leg, but it was hard for him to move one alone. Māui stood poised, the rope in his hands, and threw. Over the leg went the loop; at once he secured the rope to the wiliwili tree - and the sun was caught!

Māui brandished his magic ax and said, "Now I'm going to kill you unless you promise to travel more slowly. You don't give my mother time to get her tapa dry."

"Ow," said the sun, tugging first at one leg and then another, and rolling his huge fiery eyes toward that sharp ax. "Let me go!"

"When you promise," Māui said. "Not before." He twirled the ax around his head.

The sun looked thoughtful. "If you kill me," he said craftily after a minute, "there won't be any sunshine at all. What will your mother do then?"

Māui was silent, thinking. The sun had a good point there. At last he said, "Let's come to a bargain. If you swear that you'll go slower half the time, I'll let you go. Otherwise, you stay chained to this wiliwili tree."

"Oh, all right," sighed the sun. "I suppose I'll have to agree. I do love a good night's sleep, though." And he yawned.

"But it's time to get up now." Māui cut the sixteen strands with his ax. "Remember, slowly across the sky!"

That is how it happens that for half the year, the sun journeys slowly and we have long summer days, while for the other half he gets back to bed as quickly as he can manage.

THE SECRET OF FIRE

"This is really a great nuisance," Hina said as she put out the bananas for breakfast. "How do you suppose I managed to let my fire go out? I must be the most absent-minded woman on the island."

"It isn't so bad at breakfast-time," said Māui consolingly. "I like bananas, and coconut milk too." He took a swallow from his coconut shell. "I must say, though, that I prefer the fish to be cooked for dinner."

"Me too," chorused his four brothers.

"We're all getting tired of raw fish," went on the eldest. "If only there were something we could do about it!"

"Maybe there is," Māui said thoughtfully. "Perhaps we just have to think of what it is."

"Oh you! You're always full of bright ideas," said his brothers.

The secret of fire was lost in the mists of long-ago. Hina's mother had given her some live coals and cautioned her to keep them burning, for no one knew how to light a fire again when it had gone out. For years Hina had tended her fire-pit with care - but now, she had forgotten it, and the coals had become mere dead ashes.

That morning, when Māui was out fishing in the canoe with his brothers, he sat looking back toward Haleakalā. He was thinking deeply, and at first didn't realize what it meant when he saw a slim pillar of smoke rising from the crater at the top of the mountain. Then he gave a shout.

"There's our answer!" he cried. "Someone has a fire in the crater, and we'll go and get some of it for our mother."

"Maybe it's Pele," said one of the boys in a scared voice. They all looked dubious, except Māui.

"It can't be," he replied confidently. "Do you think the fire goddess would light such a small fire? Hers would be a volcano, with great clouds of smoke. Come, let's go!"

The boys knew that Māui was a demigod because his father, unlike their own, was a god. They were jealous of the deeds he was able to perform and belittled them, but still they were inclined to accept his word when it concerned another deity. They beached their canoe and started to walk up the mountain.

On the way they watched the column of smoke, fearful lest it disappear before they could reach it. But it was still there, scarcely moving in the quiet air, when finally they came to the great rift in the mountain's side.

They climbed up through this gap, where rivers of lava once had spilled out of the crater and down the mountainside to the sea. The smoke was just beyond a hill now, one of the volcanic cones of pinkish sand. As they walked across the rocky crater floor, it seemed to be vanishing right before their eyes ...

The boys broke into a run, and rounded the hill. There was an old 'alae hen -- scratching out the fire as fast as she could! Only embers were left.

"Wait!" cried Māui, rushing forward. "Don't put it out until you've given us a flame for our mother. Her fire has gone out."

The 'alae hen cackled to herself and kicked some sand over the last glowing coal. "Fire is my secret," she said to Māui. "I don't intend to give away either my secret or any of my coals." And she waddled off.

Discouraged and weary now after their long, fruitless climb, the boys limped down over the hills, back to their dinner of raw fish.

"The hen will light her fire again," Māui said, "and next time I'll go alone while the rest of you fish. I'll surprise her yet. Wait and see!"

Sure enough, a few days later the brothers again saw the thin spiral of smoke above the mountain top. Māui hurried up the slope and arrived panting, only to find that the hen had once more put out her fire before he could reach it. She's a smart old girl, he thought. She must have seen that there were only four boys in our canoe.

On the long downhill trek, he thought hard. When he reached home, he asked his mother for a tall calabash and a length of tapa cloth.

"Whatever do you want them for?" asked Hina, rather annoyed at being called from her tapa-making house.

"I have an idea, Ma," said Māui excitedly. "I think I know now how to outwit that old hen!" He set to work, winding the tapa around and around the calabash.

Curious, Hina stayed to watch.

Māui made a final twist of the material and said, "There! Now what does that look like? Or what would it look like if it were in a canoe with my brothers, and you saw it from the top of the mountain?"

Why -it would look just about like one of them. ''You see!" cried Māui, hugging her and swinging her around. "That's how I'm going to fool the old 'alae hen."

The next morning he placed the calabash in the canoe with his brothers and said, "You all go out fishing as usual and see what happens." He set off on the long hike.

The 'alae hen was fooled, just as he had planned, and her fire was burning brightly when Māui reached the gap in the crater's wall. How does she light it? he wondered. I'll either have to steal some coals, or find out how she does it. And I'd better learn the secret, in case Mother's fire ever goes out again.

He approached cautiously, then leaped out and grabbed the hen by the neck. "Teach me how to make a fire, old hen!" he shouted.

"Not so tight," clucked the hen, trying to wriggle free. "How can I tell you when I can scarcely breathe?"

Māui loosened his hold, and she nearly got away. "I'll have to hold you tight, if you're going to do that," he said.

She shook out her feathers as best she could and looked about, as if for help. But no one was in sight. At length she said, "All you have to do is to rub the stalk of a taro plant with a hard stick." She nodded toward a lauhala basket of wood and another of things she was going to cook.

Māui kept his grasp on her while he picked up some taro and a stick of wood, and did as she had said. No sparks came, but to this day the taro stalk has a groove in it.

Māui tightened his hold again, nearly choking the hen.

"Be careful!" she croaked. "I can hardly breathe, much less talk."

He said, "Tell me quickly!" and held her more gently.

"Try rubbing two reeds together." Nothing happened. In anger, then, he rubbed the top of that hen's head until it was red - as the 'alae hen's has been ever since.

"All right," she cackled at last. "I'll tell you because I have no other choice. You must rub a stick of hard sandalwood upon one of soft hau, and you will have fire."

Māui found these two kinds of wood in her basket, and rubbed them together. Sparks flew in all directions!

"Thank you, old hen," he said. "If you hadn't been so stubborn, I wouldn't have had to hurt you."

Down the mountainside he went with the gift of fire, making for his mother. Cooked fish for dinner! he thought as he ran.

THE GIANT EEL

When Māui's mother went for a lengthy stay on the Island of Hawai'i, he began making the long trip up Haleakalā to see his grandmother more often. He felt that she must be lonely, living at such a distance from other people - and he himself missed Hina. Besides, his grandmother always had such good things to eat! He didn't know how she managed it, for not much would grow in this rocky place, and the sea was far away. Yet she always had plenty of bananas, breadfruit, coconuts, poi, and fish of all kinds. And she made the most delicious coconut pudding!

"That's Grandma's Magic," she would reply when he asked her how she kept so well supplied, and once she added, "What are grandmothers for, if not to look out for grandchildren who come to see them?"

Māui had grown to manhood now, but he rather liked being fussed over by her; perhaps partly because he missed Hina so much. His brothers didn't often take the trouble to hike up the great mountain to see their grandmother, so he came whenever he could.

One day he brought her an ulua he had caught, and sat leaning against the trunk of the wiliwili tree while she roasted it over her coals. Later, there would be a long period in Hawai'i when men were allowed to eat nothing prepared by women. But Māui lived before this time.

His eyes were half-closed and he was almost asleep, savoring the delicious smell, when he became aware of something that made him sit up straighter. Far across the channel, above the mountains of Hawai'i, a cloud hung suspended in the air like a misty pillar.

"Grandma, look!" For some reason he couldn't explain, it frightened him to see that motionless cloud. It was unnatural. "Like an omen," he said.

His grandmother stood perfectly still as she gazed. Then she said, "It's a cry for help." She whirled about. "Be quick, Māui! That is the Ao-opua, the Warning Cloud. Your mother is in danger! Here, take the magic ax that you used in snaring the sun." She thrust it into his hands.

Māui sped down the mountain, leaping boulders, skimming over hillsides, cutting a swathe through the trees with his ax. He ran so fast that he couldn't stop until he was in the sea and the water slowed him down. Then he jumped into his canoe, and so powerfully did he paddle that in no time at all he was across the channel.

In Hilo, he was astonished to find that the Wailuku River had run dry. It was on the banks of this river that his mother was living. What could have happened? He raced up the stream-bed, springing from one large stone to another and scaling rocky cliffs over which waterfalls should be streaming.

At last, the entrance to Hina's cave! As he ran toward it, the rocks near the doorway appeared to be moving ... What was this? He then saw that his mother's ancient enemy, the giant eel Kuna Loa, was slithering over them and giving them the illusion of motion. He noticed too that below the rocks, and flowing into the cave, was a large pool of water.

That monstrous eel! He had built a dam across the river, and the entrance to Hina's cave was flooded.

With a flip of his tail, Kuna Loa swished more water into Hina's cave, and said in an oily voice, "You're too late to help your mother, Māui! She will drown." He slid into the pool. Kuna Loa had once asked Hina to marry him, and when she refused he was so angry that he swore he would get even with her.

Poor Hina! She must be wet - and terrified. Māui took time only to

call in to her, "Mother, I'm here!" Then he swung his magic ax and brought it down on the dam. At once water began to drain from Hina's cave, and to surge down the course of the stream-bed.

The big serpent slipped through the opening, and glided down through pools and over waterfalls. Māui had to run along the bank to keep up with him. As he passed hot lava rocks, he hurled them into the river; the water began to swirl and boil.

Where was that eel? Māui followed the stream down to the sea, but didn't catch another glimpse of him. Could he have hidden in some secret, rocky lair beside the river? Surely, thought Māui, gazing upstream, Kuna Loa must have been cooked in that steaming water.

He made his way back to the cave and called, "It's all right, Mother! Come on out. Kuna Loa is gone."

Hina appeared at the cave's entrance, shaking out her long, wet hair. "Oh, how good it is to feel sunshine again!" she said. "Thank you, my son. You have saved me."

"Mother," said Māui, taking hold of her arms, "when are you coming home? I miss you."

"I'll come, don't worry," she said. "But not quite yet. Now just help me to dry out my cave."

Back on his own island, Māui went to his grandmother's to tell her what had happened. "You should have seen that huge eel," he said, shuddering. "He was hideous."

"I've seen the nasty creature," she replied. "Good riddance, if he's really gone!"

"Grandmother," he said, "why doesn't my mother come home?"

His grandmother was silent for a moment. Then she said gently, "She's a roving soul, Māui. Think of all the places she's lived in."

"She told me she would come," he persisted.

"Perhaps..." But then she lifted her head, listening, and clutched his arm. "Māui, do you hear that?" A faint wailing sound was borne to them by the trade winds.

Māui stood very still, listening too. "It is my mother," he said, "uttering a chant of fear. She is in trouble again." As swiftly as before, he journeyed to Hawai'i. His mother, feeling secure now, had wandered some distance from her cave. When he found her, she was running in terror from Kuna Loa, who lashed through the grass behind her. She leapt into a breadfruit tree and clung to its branches - while the eel's great slimy body wound itself about the trunk of the tree.

"Oh, Māui!" she cried piteously.

"He won't escape this time," Māui said.

The eel began to uncoil himself from the tree in an effort to escape, but Māui wasted no time in aiming a blow at him with the magic ax. He flourished it aloft, and struck again and again. The great moist body was cut into a thousand pieces. It is said that these bits found their way back to the river, where they became the eels that are found in it today.

"Come, Mother." Māui held up his hands to help Hina from the breadfruit tree. When she was safely on the ground, he held her still and asked, "When are you coming home, where I can take proper care of you?"

"Someday," she said lightly. "Someday I'll come."

He stood watching her as she went back toward her cave.

THE SECRET OF IMMORTALITY

(adapted from the Māori legend)

Māui watched the moon, month by month, lose its fullness and slowly become but a crescent bright on the night sky. At last, when it was so slim that it seemed it must disappear, he saw it begin to grow again in size. Each day, he watched as the sun rose and traveled in fiery splendor across the sky, then sank beyond the horizon, leaving blackness behind. Yet, in the morning, there it was rising again. The stars seemed at times to vanish, but always they returned to spangle the sky.

Why is it, he wondered, that when man dies, he is gone forever from his earthly home? Why should man not be immortal, even as the sun and the moon.

Māui sought the god who was his father, and asked him these questions. His father said: "Only the Guardian of the Night, she who is called Hina-nui-te-po, knows the secret of immortality. You have performed great deeds, my son, but this you can never know. It's better not to think about these things."

But Māui's imagination had been caught, and he could not help wondering. "Where does this goddess live, Father?" he asked.

His father showed him the island where Hina-nui-te-po lived, but warned him that none could pass her guards, standing upright as a man does.

Māui swam to the island and crept silently past the guards on his hands and knees. He entered the palace, and returned to his brothers with food belonging to the goddess.

They were terrified and said, "Māui, you have done wonderful things. We admit it, even though we have teased you at times. Perhaps we were only jealous. But please, Māui, leave the great goddess alone and stay with us."

Māui could not forget his desire, however, to learn for himself and his people the secret of life.

"I must go, brothers," he said. "When Hina-nui-te-po is asleep, I shall enter her body and find the answer to immortality. If I can bring it back with me, it will mean that no man must die. Which of you will go with me?"

The brothers were afraid and did not want to go. They tried to dissuade Māui.

"We will all be killed, Māui," they said. "And what will be the use? It is better for us to live out the spans of our lives. Think of our families, if we should all be gone."

"Think of all mankind, if I should solve the mystery!" he replied.

The brothers shook their heads; they did not like the plan.

"I don't want to go," said one.

"Nor I," agreed another.

"I have an idea," said Māui. "I'll transform you all into birds of different kinds. You may be able to help me, and I want you there. But if the danger becomes too great, you can simply fly away."

The brothers decided that this would be safe enough, and since Māui was determined to go, they said they would accompany him. So Māui affected the transformations.

"But remember, he cautioned," you must make no sound until I am safely out of the goddess' body." The birds twittered in agreement, and Māui looked at them anxiously. It was so easy for a bird to twitter! "Do be careful," he pleaded. "It's most important. You especially, 'Elepaio. It's hard for you to be still, I know, but you must. As soon as I have left the goddess' body, you may chatter all you want. Then she will be dead and man will live forever!"

They could see Hina-nui-te-po on her island, far across the water. As the sun set beyond her, she glittered with light, as if a golden halo stood out about her. She is very beautiful, thought Māui.

When darkness had fallen and the goddess had retired for the night, he swam back to her island, the birds fluttering above him. The goddess was asleep when they reached her abode. Her large, fishlike mouth was open.

Māui warned his brothers against making any noise and, with his spear, leapt into her throat. Down he went, into her stomach, and there he found what he longed for: the secret of immortality.

He returned to her mouth, bearing the prize, and was about to jump to the ground when the 'elepaio burst into a sudden shrill chattering. Hina-nui-te-po awoke, and her teeth cut Māui in two.

Thus was the secret of life lost to mankind, and thus did Māui die.

> "But death is nothing new
>
> Death is, and has been ever since old Māui died
>
> Then Pata-tai laughed loud
>
> And woke the goblin-god
>
> Who severed him in two, and shut him in,
>
> So dusk of eve came on." -Māori Death Chant

49

GLOSSARY

ʻalae: Endemic waterfowl. Hawaiian common moorhen, mudhen, or ʻalae ʻula ("burnt forehead")

ʻelepaio: A species of flycatcher, the ʻelepaio is the first native bird to sing in the morning and the last to stop singing at night.

hala: *Pandanus tectorius*. An indigenous tree. Leaves are used for weaving mats, sails, thatch. Fruit for lei, dye brushes. Roots for cordage, medicine.

hau: A lowland tree. The light, tough wood is used for canoe outriggers, the bast for rope, the sap and flowers for medicine.

kauila: A native tree, its hard wood was used for spears and tools.

koa: A tree of the acacia family. Its wood is used for canoes, surfboards, calabashes.

lauhala: Pandanus leaf, woven into mats, pillows, baskets, sails.

lei: Garland, wreath.

malo: A boy's or man's loincloth.

pili: A native grass used for thatching houses.

Pimoe: In Hawaiian mythology, a giant ulua, god of fishes.

poi: The Hawaiian staff of life, usually made from taro root that was baked in an underground oven and pounded with water.

tapa or kapa: A cloth made from the inner bark of trees such as mulberry, and used for clothes and bedclothes.

taro or kalo: A staple Hawaiian food source. The root is used to make poi; the leaves for luau, a vegetable similar to spinach.

ulua: Giant trevally or jack. A large ocean fish. Important Hawaiian food source.

wiliwili: A species of flowering tree found in dry lowland forests. Its very light wood is used for surfboards, canoe outriggers and fishnet floats. The red seeds are used in lei.

LIST of ILLUSTRATIONS

*Reproductions available at www.DietrichVarez.com or
Volcano Art Center www.VolcanoArtCenter.org*

ABOUT THE AUTHOR

Barbara Baldwin Lyons, a descendant of some of the earliest missionaries to the islands, was born in Honolulu in 1912. The middle child of Samuel Alexander Baldwin, who managed the Haleakalā Ranch Co. Ltd. and Haleakalā Dairy, she grew up on the ranch, becoming a skilled horsewoman and a voracious reader. Her deeply engraved love of Hawai'i and the Hawaiian culture sprang from her family's deep roots, extending back to the 1840s. She lived most of her life on Māui except when her husband, retired Rear Admiral Raymond R. Lyons, was serving in the U.S. Navy. An avid student of Hawaiian folklore, Lyons shared her passion in two books and a column that she wrote for years in the Māui News. She passed away on Māui in 2001 at the age of 89.

ABOUT THE ILLUSTRATOR

Dietrich Varez was born in Berlin, Germany in 1939. He came to live in Hawai'i at the age of eight, growing up island-style on Oahu, exploring the land and sea, and absorbing a love of Hawaiian culture and storytelling. After earning a BA in English Literature at UH Mānoa he and his wife Linda, a fellow artist moved to the island of Hawai'i. They settled in Volcano with their young son in 1968. A self-taught artist and avid student of Hawaiian and Polynesian folklore, he turned to carving linoleum blocks to tell the stories and myths of Hawai'i. His signature brown ink prints are instantly recognizable. He also designed fabrics for Reyn Spooner aloha shirts and created many paintings of the volcano, plants, wildlife and especially the goddess, Pele. He passed away in 2018 at the age of 79. The Volcano Art Center, of which he was a founding member, has dedicated the Dietrich Varez Hall at their Naiulani Campus to his memory.

Books published by
PETROGLYPH PRESS

A CONCISE HISTORY OF
THE HAWAIIAN ISLANDS
by Phil K. Barnes

HAWAIIAN LEGENDS
OF VOLCANOES
by William D. Westervelt
illustrations by Dietrich Varez

HILO LEGENDS
by Frances Reed

HINA - THE GODDESS
by Dietrich Varez

IʻA,
SEALIFE COLORING BOOK
by Jan Moon

ʻIWA,
THE HAWAIIAN LEGEND
by Dietrich Varez

KĀNEHŪNAMŌKU
by Dietrich Varez

KONA LEGENDS
by Eliza D. Maguire

LEGENDS OF MĀUI
by William D. Westervelt
illustrations by Dietrich Varez

MĀUI, MISCHIEVOUS HERO
by Barbara Baldwin Lyons
illustrations by Dietrich Varez

PELE AND HIʻIAKA,
A TALE OF TWO SISTERS
by Dietrich Varez

PELE, VOLCANO GODDESS
OF HAWAIʻI
by Likeke R. McBride
illustrations by Dietrich Varez

PETROGLYPHS OF HAWAIʻI
by Likeke R. McBride

PLANTS OF HAWAIʻI -
HOW TO GROW THEM
by Fortunato Teho

PRACTICAL FOLK
MEDICINE OF HAWAIʻI
by Likeke R. McBride

STARS OVER HAWAIʻI
by E. H. Bryan, Jr. &
Richard Crowe

THE LIFE AND TIMES
OF KAMEHAMEHA
by William D. Westervelt
iIllustrations by Dietrich Varez

THE STORY OF LAUHALA
by Edna W. Stall

TROPICAL ORGANIC
GARDENING,
HAWAIIAN STYLE
by Richard L. Stevens